The Magic Moscow

overleaf:
my boss,
Steve Nickelson

The Magic Moscow

BY DANIEL PINKWATER

ALADDIN BOOKS
Macmillan Publishing Company   NEW YORK
Maxwell Macmillan Canada   TORONTO
Maxwell Macmillan International
NEW YORK   OXFORD   SINGAPORE   SYDNEY

Any resemblance to persons or dogs living or dead is
purely coincidental.

First Aladdin Books edition 1993
Copyright © 1980 by Daniel Pinkwater

Aladdin Books   Maxwell Macmillan Canada, Inc.
Macmillan Publishing Company   1200 Eglinton Avenue East
866 Third Avenue   Suite 200
New York, NY 10022   Don Mills, Ontario M3C 3N1

Macmillan Publishing Company is part of the Maxwell
Communication Group of Companies.

Printed in the United States of America

10 9 8 7 6 5 4 3 2 1

Library of Congress Cataloging-in-Publication Data
Pinkwater, Daniel Manus, 1941–
   The Magic Moscow / by Daniel Pinkwater.—1st
Aladdin Books ed.
     p. cm.
   Summary: Relates the adventures of Edward, grand-
son of a famous television sled dog, with his owner
Steve, who manages a Hoboken ice cream stand.
   ISBN 0-689-71710-5
   [1. Dogs—Fiction. 2. Humorous stories.] I. Title.
PZ7.P6335Mai   1993
[Fic]—dc20   92-27150

to Tsuya

1

EVERYBODY KNOWS what a Magic Moocow is. They're everywhere. They're those soft ice cream stands — the ones with the big plaster sculpture of a cow's head on top. There used to be a Magic Moocow in Hoboken, but it was taken over by my friend Steve Nickelson. He changed it into the Magic Moscow, by painting out the second "o" in Moocow and painting in an "s." He also painted the cow's head with diagonal purple and orange stripes.

Steve Nickelson is my friend. He's also my boss. I have a part-time job at the Magic Moscow. In the summer, I work full-time.

It's interesting working for Steve. He's a big guy with a bushy brown beard. He always wears a white shirt with the tail hanging out. On the tail is a black stamp that says "Bandini's Linen Service – Union City, N.J." He wears white pants from Bandini's, too. He never wears anything else — even when he's not working — even when he's wandering around the streets of Hoboken.

Steve is a collector. He collects any number of things. He collects comic books: he has almost a half-million of them. He collects old records. He has a lot of them, too. He collects old pennies. He collects bottlecaps. He collects antique sneakers and basketball shoes. Once he started a collection of twigs and small sticks. He put advertisements in newspapers all over the country, and people sent him twigs and small sticks. Another collection he started was beans. He tried to get one of every kind of bean on earth.

Steve tends to get tired of the little collections, like antique sneakers, twigs, and beans. The ones he really works on are the comics, old records, science-fiction books, and old magazines.

My part-time job is helping Steve in the Magic Moscow, but sometimes I help him with his collections. Sometimes, I just sit around in the Magic Moscow, after closing time, looking through comics with Steve and listening to old records. He keeps a lot of his collections in the back of the store.

This particular summer, Steve went on a Sergeant Schwartz of the Yukon kick. Sergeant Schwartz of the Yukon is a Canadian mountie. He always gets his man. And he has this smart dog. The dog's name is Hercules. That's the name of the television program, "Sergeant Schwartz of the Yukon and His Great Dog Hercules." It's an old program. It isn't on regular TV anymore. Steve got in the habit of leaving work at three-thirty every day to watch reruns on UHF. He also started collecting *Sergeant Schwartz of the Yukon and His Great Dog Hercules* comic books. He read them all the time. Once he found a Sergeant Schwartz record. He also got some posters — old ones — and his dearest wish was to see one of the *Sergeant Schwartz of the Yukon and His Great Dog Hercules* movies that they made years ago.

All the time, Steve used to whistle the theme song from "Sergeant Schwartz of the Yukon and His Great Dog Hercules."

He really loved Sergeant Schwartz of the

Yukon — and he really loved the great dog Hercules.

After a while, it appeared to me that Steve loved the great dog Hercules even more than Sergeant Schwartz. Every time a big dog, like a German shepherd, went by the Magic Moscow Steve would watch it until it was out of sight. Sometimes, when he was cleaning out the giant soft-ice-cream machines, I would hear Steve having an imaginary conversation: "Get up, you huskies — Get up, Hercules," he would say under his breath. And he'd make barking and woofing noises, too.

It was only a matter of time.

In the back of an old copy of *Sergeant Schwartz of the Yukon and His Great Dog Hercules: Comics and Stories*, Steve found an advertisement:

Boys and girls! You can have a real
ALASKAN MALAMUTE
Just like Sergeant Schwartz's great dog
HERCULES!!!!!!!!
Gold Rush Kennels, Nutley, New Jersey

It was an old magazine, but the Gold Rush Kennels were still there: Steve made sure by telephoning. Then he started locking up the Magic Moscow. "Come on, Norman," he said to me, "we're going to look at some dogs!"

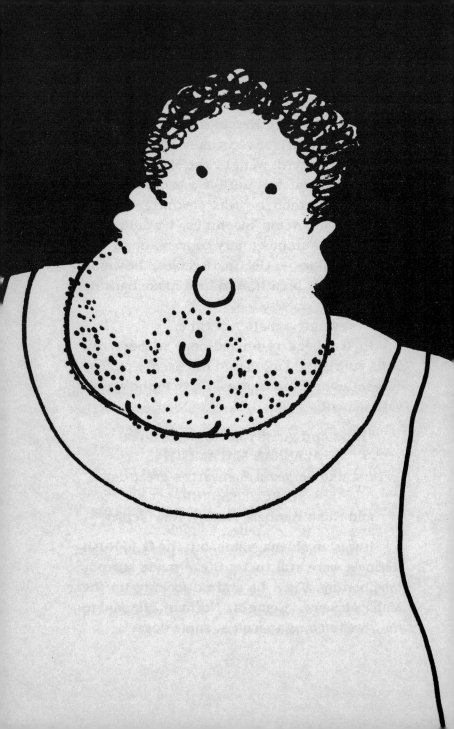

2

WE PILED into Steve's little car and took off. About an hour later, we pulled up in front of the Gold Rush Kennels in Nutley, New Jersey. It was just an ordinary house. The only thing that told us it was a kennel was the sign in front.

We rang the bell. A big fat guy in his undershirt came to the door. He was smoking a cigarette, and he needed a shave.

"How do you do," the big fat guy said. "I am John Crisco, the proprietor of Gold Rush Kennels. Are you the gentleman who called?"

"I'm Steve Nickelson," Steve said, "and this is my friend, Norman Bleistift."

John Crisco smelled of after-shave or deodorant. He had oily stuff in his hair. "And how may I help you?" he asked.

"Well, we thought we'd like to look at your dogs, if that's all right with you," Steve said.

"Look?" John Crisco said. "Of course you can look. That's no problem. You can look, sure. Look all you want. But I hope you aren't planning to buy a puppy. My puppies are not for sale to just anybody. Only very special people can buy my puppies. I have to know a lot about you before you take a puppy away from here. So you can look, but don't think I'm going to sell you a puppy."

John Crisco took us by the hands and led us out the back door.

In the yard, there were dogs in rows of cages. When they saw us, they went wild. They barked and wagged their tails, and they stood up with their front feet on the wire doors of their cages.

The place was dirty. It smelled.

"Please pardon the appearance of this place," John Crisco said. "The boy who cleans up got sick today, and I haven't had a chance to tidy up."

Steve didn't hear him. All the dogs looked more or less like Sergeant Schwartz's great dog Hercules, and Steve was fascinated.

Steve walked up and down in front of the cages. Sometimes he would stop and look at a puppy. "Ooooh, I like this one," he would say, or "This one is cute." The puppies were going crazy. I guess they were hoping that Steve would take them out of those dirty cages and give them a home.

"I can see you know a lot about dogs," John Crisco said. "The puppies you seem to like are the very best ones. Some of them are almost as good as Platinum Blazing Yukon Flash."

"Platinum Blazing Yukon Flash?" Steve asked.

"Yes, the finest puppy I've seen in many a year," John Crisco said. "His grandfather was the dog who played Sergeant Schwartz's dog, Hercules, on television — you know, Sergeant Schwartz of the Yukon. The grandfather's name was Champion Goldentooth Gorilla."

"Gosh," Steve said, "Sergeant Schwartz's dog's grandson! Is he here? Could we see him?"

"Aha!" John Crisco shouted. "I knew it all along! You want to get me to sell him to you. You didn't fool me by pretending you had never heard of him! Shame on you, trying to trick me like that!"

"Mr. Crisco, I'm not trying to trick you," Steve said. "I'd just like to have a look at him. Is he really the grandson of the great dog Hercules, I mean, Champion Goldentooth Gorilla?"

"I'll never let him go!" John Crisco shouted. "It doesn't matter that I'm poor and have all these other dogs to feed and take care of. I will keep Platinum Blazing Yukon Flash — somehow. Somehow, I will find a way to keep him and take him to dog shows, so he can win ribbons and become a famous champion. I don't know how I'll manage it, but I'll do it!" John Crisco was crying. He threw his big fat body to the ground, made little moaning noises, and beat on the ground with his fists and feet.

"There, there, Mr. Crisco," Steve said, "I didn't mean to upset you." John Crisco paid no attention: he continued to moan and drum on the ground. "We'll just be going now," Steve said. "We only wanted to have a look." Steve started to move away from John Crisco.

"Look? Of course you may look." John Crisco sprang to his feet. It was surprising to see such a fat man move so quickly. "Just remember, he's not for sale."

John Crisco took a padlock off the door to his garage. "I don't keep him in with the ordinary dogs," he said.

It was dark in the garage. Out of the shadows came a funny-looking puppy, blinking in the sunlight. I put out my hand, and he licked it. He smelled of the same after-shave that John Crisco used. Someone had brushed him recently — I could tell, because his hair was parted in the middle, just like John Crisco's.

"That's Platinum Blazing Yukon Flash?" Steve asked.

"Well, I just call him Edward for short," John Crisco said.

"But he looks kind of scrawny and sickly," Steve said. "His head is too big and his feet are floppy and he's coughing."

John Crisco slapped Steve on the back. "Now, don't tease. We real dog fanciers should be honest with one another. I was watching you in the kennels, and I can see that you know a good dog when you see one. Either you're an expert — or, even better, a natural genius when it comes to dogs. Now, tell me, doesn't he look exactly like his grandfather, Champion Goldentooth Gorilla?"

Steve squinted and put his head sideways, looking at the puppy, who was now sitting down and blinking — once he sneezed. "Isn't he kind of small?" Steve asked.

"He's big for his size," John Crisco said. "Just feel him."

John Crisco lifted the puppy and handed him to Steve. The puppy licked his face. "I guess I see what you mean. I guess he is sort of big for his size."

"This is the greatest puppy I've ever raised," John Crisco said. "When he grows up, he'll be a famous Alaskan Malamute and win ribbons and trophies and be a great champion. All my life I've hoped to someday have a dog as good as this one will be. I'll tell you something about this dog, I've decided to give him to you."

"What?" Steve shouted. "You want to give him to me? Your best dog ever? Platinum Blazing Yukon Flash?"

"Yes," John Crisco said, "he belongs with someone who can really take care of him and give him every advantage. I know you will take Edward — I call him Edward for short, you know — to lots of dog shows and help him to become a famous champion."

John Crisco was crying again. The puppy had jumped into Steve's arms and was licking his face, and John Crisco was hugging them both.

"But I can't just take him away," Steve said. "I can't just accept the best puppy you ever had as a gift."

"Well, if it will make you feel any better about it," John Crisco said, "you can give me three hundred dollars for him."

John Crisco counted the money three times, before we loaded Edward, also known as Platinum Blazing Yukon Flash, into Steve's little car.

As we drove away, John Crisco waved to us and kissed the bundle of bills from time to time.

3

EVEN THOUGH Steve is technically an adult, he still lives with his mother and father. When he introduced Edward to them, they told him that Edward was not invited to live in their house. You really couldn't blame them. Large portions of Steve's comic book, record, and sneaker collections — those things that wouldn't fit in the back room of the Magic Moscow — were already in the house and his mother and father hardly had room to move around.

So we tried taking Edward to live at my house. My parents were very unfair. They just said no, without any really good reason, except that they're both allergic to dogs.

So Edward went to live in the Magic Moscow.

The after-shave lotion that John Crisco had squirted him with was beginning to wear off, and Edward smelled pretty stale. We gave him three baths, which helped a little. After his baths, Edward crawled under a table and went to sleep.

"Are you sure that he's going to be a famous show dog?" I asked.

"Of course he is," Steve said. "He looks just like his grandfather, Champion Goldentooth Gorilla. Didn't you see how John Crisco hated to part with him? When he grows up, he will be a famous dog and win lots of ribbons."

Edward coughed in his sleep under the table.

"Then why didn't John Crisco keep him?" I asked. We looked at Edward. His head was too big for his body, and his feet were floppy. When he walked around, he kept bumping into things.

We took Edward to the vet, who gave him some medicine for his cough. The vet said he was not a very healthy puppy, but if we took extra good care of him and fed him well, he might grow up to be big and strong.

Edward liked living in the Magic Moscow. He liked Steve and me. He liked getting all the food and water he wanted. Every night Steve would make him a grilled cheese sandwich, as a special treat, before we went home. Edward's cough got better.

We expected him to get bigger, but we weren't prepared for how fast he got bigger and how big he got. He got to be *very* big *very* fast. His head got bigger, too; but he still kept tripping and bumping into things because his feet were still too big for his body.

Edward liked the people who came to the Magic Moscow. When someone he especially liked came, he would jump up and down, trip and fall down, and lick their faces. At other times, he would lie behind the counter asleep, snoring and growling. Even after months of baths, he still had a faint smell like very old basketball shoes.

For a long time, Edward was afraid of trucks. Whenever one went past, he would shriek and jump in the air.

Edward got over being afraid of trucks. Then he took up singing. He usually sang at night, and the people who lived near the Magic Moscow would call Steve on the telephone and make suggestions about Edward.

For a long time, Edward went through a period of liking to fight with other dogs. Whenever Edward saw another dog, he would try to chomp it. He especially wanted to fight big dogs, and Steve or I would have to drag him away, snarling and growling. Steve thought that maybe Edward had had a bad experience when he was little.

Steve didn't know how right he was. One day a customer came to the Magic Moscow. His name was Davis Davis, and he was a world-famous dog expert. He told us so.

"That looks like one of John Crisco's Malamutes," Davis Davis said.

"That's right," Steve said. "Can you tell just by looking?"

"Friend, there's very little I don't know about dogs," Davis Davis said, "and I know quite a bit about the famous Mr. John Crisco, too."

"Such as what?" Steve asked.

"Well, for one thing, he doesn't feed his dogs enough. He doesn't give them enough water either, which is even meaner. And he doesn't take them to the vet. If they get sick, they just get better on their own — or else."

"Or else?" Steve asked.

"Or else." Davis Davis continued, "John Crisco is mean to all his dogs but one. That is the only really good dog he has — at least he thinks so. See, he has this gigantic Malamute named Prince Razorback of Mukamuk. He must weigh two hundred pounds. He's the biggest Malamute that ever lived — also the meanest. He lives in John Crisco's own house, mostly under the kitchen sink, thinking evil thoughts. He sleeps in John Crisco's own bed. John Crisco feeds him Hershey bars, which is the only reason he has never bitten John Crisco. That dog loves Hershey bars. Say, could I have one of those Moron's Delights?"

The Moron's Delight is one of Steve's specialties. It has six flavors of ice cream — two scoops of each — a banana, a carrot, three kinds of syrup, whole roasted peanuts, a slice of Swiss cheese, a radish, yogurt, wheat germ, and a kosher pickle. It is served in a shoebox lined with plastic wrap. Steve considers it a health-food dessert.

While Steve was making the Moron's Delight, Davis Davis went on about John Crisco: "At night, John Crisco lets Prince Razorback of Mukamuk go out to the kennels and terrify the dogs and puppies, poor things. If Prince Razorback of Mukamuk sees a nose or a paw sticking out of a cage, he just chomps it. He's a nasty dog.

"Every now and then, John Crisco takes Prince Razorback to a dog show," Davis Davis went on. "He touches him up with a fountain pen, squirts a lot of after-shave lotion on him, and takes him out to win a blue ribbon. Of course he usually scares the judges so badly that he wins. But the really interesting thing about John Crisco is the way he can sell dogs. He makes up all sorts of high-sounding names for them and gets people to pay six times what the dog is worth. One of his favorite tricks is telling people that a dog is the grandson of Sergeant Schwartz's dog, Hercules. Well, first of all, Hercules was never a Malamute in the first place: he was a Saint Bernard with a lot of makeup. Also, he never did have any puppies. Yes, sir, that John Crisco is quite an operator."

Davis Davis walked away, eating his Moron's Delight with a plastic spoon as he went.

"Do you think he's right?" I asked Steve. "Do you think that John Crisco is a swindler?"

"No," Steve said. "That Davis Davis doesn't know everything."

Then he looked at Edward for a long time.

"You know," Steve said, "even if Edward doesn't become a famous champion and win prizes at dog shows, he's a very nice dog, just the same."

"I think so, too," I said.

That night Steve put a scoop of ice cream on top of Edward's grilled cheese sandwich.

4

NATURALLY, we use a lot of milk at the Magic Moscow. The guy who sells us the milk is a friend of Steve's. His name is Bruce, and he's an interesting person. The most interesting thing about Bruce is Cheryl, his horse. Bruce says she's the last horse in Hoboken. Bruce brings the milk in a horse-drawn milk wagon.

Cheryl pulls it, of course. Cheryl is the only horse I know. She's a real old horse. She's white with pink around her wrinkled old nose and watery brown eyes.

Bruce is always talking about what a smart horse Cheryl is. I never saw her do anything to show that she's smart. I mean, she's a nice horse, and I always used to go outside when Bruce delivered the milk and feed Cheryl some stale bread — and she'd sort of snort and nuzzle me — but that doesn't go to show any special intelligence.

Usually when Bruce would come by with the milk, he'd sit around in the Magic Moscow, having a bowl of soup and telling Steve how smart his horse was. He said that Cheryl had correctly predicted the outcome of the last five presidential elections. I never heard her say a word.

When Edward came to live at the Magic Moscow, the conversations between Steve and Bruce changed. Bruce would still brag about how smart his horse was, but now Steve had an animal to brag about. He'd tell Bruce how smart Edward was. He'd also talk about Edward's famous grandfather, Champion Goldentooth Gorilla, the dog who played Sergeant Schwartz of the Yukon's dog on television.

Meanwhile, Edward fell in love with Cheryl. He thought she was the most wonderful thing he'd ever seen. The first time Bruce and Cheryl came by, after we'd just brought Edward to the Magic Moscow, Edward went crazy. He whined and barked and jumped up and down at the window.

We took Edward outside and introduced him to the horse. He licked Cheryl's nose, and she nuzzled him and made little grunting noises.

After that, Cheryl would whinny for Edward. Edward would bark and whine and howl until we let him out. Then he'd cavort on the sidewalk, giving Cheryl kisses on the nose, and Cheryl would reach down and bump Edward lovingly.

Sometimes we'd let Edward go off with Bruce and Cheryl. He'd ride in the milk wagon, smiling and wagging his tail and barking.

Not far from the Magic Moscow is a park where Steve and I would take Edward for exercise. One day there was a sign posted in the park saying that the Hoboken Sled Dog Club was going to have its annual show in that very park on the following Saturday. We decided we'd enter Edward — just for fun.

We didn't know it, but early in the morning on that following Saturday, John Crisco got up extra early. He fed all the dogs at Gold Rush Kennels in Nutley, New Jersey, and then he coaxed Prince Razorback out from under the sink by offering him Hershey bars.

John Crisco put an extra lot of oily stuff on his hair and squirted himself and Prince Razorback of Mukamuk all over with after-shave lotion. John Crisco also put on his special lucky shirt he had brought back from Florida and touched up Prince Razorback's fur here and there with a fountain pen.

John Crisco coaxed Prince Razorback of Mukamuk into the back seat of his car, again by offering him Hershey bars. Then, wearing his special lucky shirt, his sunglasses, and his white tennis shoes, John Crisco started out for the Hoboken Sled Dog Club's annual show.

When Steve and I arrived with Edward, the park was already full of Malamutes. There were big ones and small ones, tall ones and short ones, black and white ones, gray ones, red ones, brown ones, tough ones, silly ones. There were dozens and dozens of Malamutes, with pink tongues flapping, tails wagging, barking and howling, growling and whining, and squeaking and mumbling.

Malamutes like other Malamutes better than anything. They like to play with each other, show off for each other, and pick fights with each other. Edward had never seen so many Malamutes since his days at Gold Rush Kennels of Nutley, New Jersey.

He just stood there for a while, figuring it out. Then he began to wag his tail.

"I don't think he sees anybody that he wants to fight with," I said.

"I'm sure Edward will behave," Steve said. "I'll go and enter him in the dog show now."

"I'm going to walk around," I said. "I'll catch up with you later."

There were rings, like boxing rings, set up for the dogs to be shown in. There was a table with silver cups and little statues, the prizes that would go to the winners. Next to that was a table where people, wearing ribbons that said "OFFICIAL," were writing down the names of the dogs that were entered in the show. Steve told them to write down Platinum Blazing Yukon Flash, and they gave him a cardboard number to wear on his arm.

"Go to ring number three, and wait for your number to be called," one of the officials told Steve.

John Crisco arrived with Prince Razorback of Mukamuk. He had a hard time persuading Prince Razorback to get out of the car. After eating six Hershey bars, Prince Razorback finally decided to get out and go with John Crisco to the tables where the officials were taking down names. All the way from the car to the official's table, Prince Razorback made a low growling noise in his throat and looked from side to side as people and dogs got out of his way.

"Go to ring number three and wait for your number to be called," the official told John Crisco. John Crisco and Prince Razorback went to ring number three, where Steve and Edward were waiting. John Crisco had forgotten Steve and Edward, and Steve was waving to me on the other side of the ring, so he didn't see John Crisco. But apparently Edward remembered John Crisco — and he especially remembered Prince Razorback of Mukamuk. Edward also remembered that he was a big dog now.

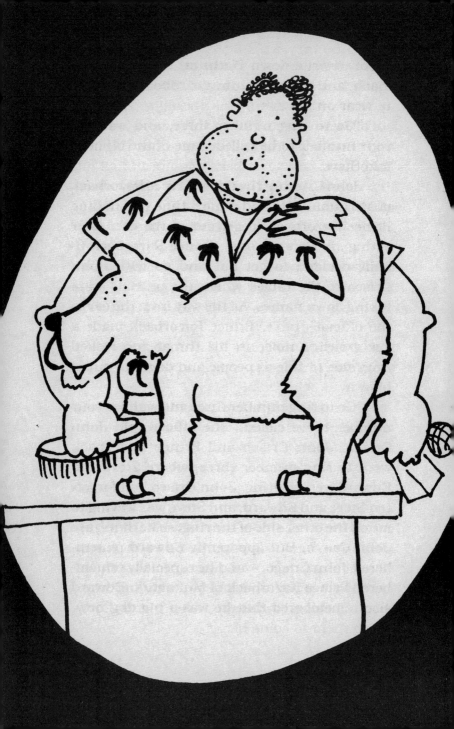

And he remembered all the practice he'd had trying to chomp dogs around Hoboken.

Edward lunged forward, pulling his leash out of Steve's hand. He ran at Prince Razorback and chomped him on the nose – hard. Prince Razorback had never been chomped in all his life. He was so big that dogs had always been afraid of him. He had done all the chomping. Prince Razorback wasn't exactly scared, but he was so surprised that he did a backward somersault and started running. Edward ran after him, growling and screaming.

When Prince Razorback started to run he broke the heavy chain that was attached to his collar, and John Crisco fell over backward, on top of Steve who was just turning around to see what had happened.

John Crisco and Steve struggled to their feet and began running after their dogs, shouting to them to come back.

Edward chased Prince Razorback all around the park. When some of the dogs saw Prince Razorback running straight at them, they got scared, broke away, and started running from him. Some of the other dogs saw Prince Razorback and Edward run past them, and broke away and started running after them. The dogs' owners ran after them, shouting to them to come back.

There were soon one hundred and twenty-two dogs, including Prince Razorback and Edward, running as fast as they could around the park: sixty dogs running away from Prince Razorback, sixty-one dogs, including Edward, running after him. And there were one hundred and twenty-two owners, including John Crisco and Steve, running after them.

Prince Razorback was not very bright. He didn't have many ideas, but as he was running, he started to have one: "Why Prince Razorback run from all stupid little dogs?" he thought. "Better Prince Razorback chase *them*." Prince Razorback of Mukamuk stopped and turned around. He made an awful face and ran at the dogs who had been running after him. All the dogs screamed and started running the other way — all except Edward, who stood still and got ready to fight. But Prince Razorback had forgotten all about Edward's chomping him on the nose. He was interested in chasing the sixty-one dogs who had been chasing him. He crashed right into Edward and ran over him.

When the one hundred and twenty-two owners saw half the dogs running toward them, they started waving their arms and shouting, "Here, girl!" "Come, boy!" They tried to catch their dogs, but the dogs slipped past them.

The dogs who had not been running after Prince Razorback stopped when they noticed that no one was chasing them anymore. Then they saw all the dogs running in the opposite direction — away from Prince Razorback — and started running after them. They ran right over Edward, who was just getting over being knocked down by Prince Razorback.

There was a little lake in the park, and Prince Razorback chased the dogs who were running away from him right into it. Then he jumped in after them. Once they were in the water, the dogs forgot about chasing and being chased. Even Prince Razorback calmed down and floated on his back, waving his paws in the air.

All the owners lined up on the edge of the little lake and shouted to their dogs to come back. Then the other bunch of dogs, the ones who had been running away from Prince Razorback and then turned around, arrived at the edge of the lake, going fast. They bumped into the crowd of owners and knocked most of them into the water. Then the dogs jumped in, too.

I found Edward, walking in circles, shaking his head to get over being knocked down twice and run over by one hundred and twenty-one Malamutes. Steve came along, dripping, and picked up Edward's leash and led him back to ring number three, where the judge was waiting.

In the lake the owners were splashing around, trying to catch their dogs and drag them up the muddy, slippery bank.

Edward won a blue ribbon — also a red ribbon, a yellow ribbon, and a white ribbon. He won six silver cups, too, because every other dog was soaking wet, covered with mud, or still swimming in the lake.

It was late afternoon when we took Edward back to the Magic Moscow, along with the blue, red, yellow, and white ribbons and the six silver cups.

Most of the other dogs had been caught and taken home. Some of the owners were drying off their dogs with towels. John Crisco was tired after all the running and swimming, and he and Prince Razorback were floating on their backs, eating some Hershey bars that John Crisco had in his pockets.

"I think Edward did very well for his first time," Steve said.

"Me, too," I said. "I'm sure he would have won even if all the other dogs hadn't jumped in the lake."

Steve arranged all of Edward's trophies and ribbons over the counter at the Magic Moscow. He made Edward a Moron's Delight to celebrate his winning.

When customers came to the Magic Moscow, they asked Steve, "Did your dog win all those ribbons and trophies?"

"Of course he did," Steve said. "He's a very important dog. He is the grandson of Champion Goldentooth Gorilla, the dog that played Hercules, Sergeant Schwartz of the Yukon's dog. His name is Platinum Blazing Yukon Flash, but we just call him Edward."

5

AFTER A WHILE, things began to quiet down. Steve had bragged to everybody in town, and Edward had wandered off to nap in the alley behind the Magic Moscow. Steve spent a lot of time looking at the trophies and ribbons. He was really happy.

Bruce the milkman came by, without Cheryl, and Steve told him how Edward had beaten four hundred Malamutes at the dog show. Every time he told the story, he'd add a few dogs to the number to make the competition seem stiffer.

Bruce the milkman was a little jealous, I could tell. Even though he claimed Cheryl was the smartest horse in the world, it would be too farfetched to claim that she had ever been in, much less won, a horse show. Still, he tried to be a good sport, and he congratulated Steve.

While Steve and Bruce the milkman were talking, a stranger came into the Magic Moscow. He was tall and neat looking, with one of those thin mustaches. He had high boots on and a sort of cowboy hat.

When Steve saw the stranger, his mouth dropped open, and his eyes opened wide.

"Excuse me," said the stranger, "I'm trying to find the park. There's supposed to be a dog show today, and I'm afraid I've missed it. The traffic on the New Jersey Turnpike was just awful."

Steve was trying to talk. He couldn't seem to get any words to come out. He just went, "Uh . . . uh . . . uh . . . uh."

Finally Steve managed to get himself together. "It's Sergeant Schwartz!" he shouted. "It's Sergeant Schwartz of the Yukon! Right here! In my store!" Then he fainted.

He didn't actually faint all the way, out cold on the floor. He just staggered and had to grab the counter for support.

"Are you all right, old man?" Sergeant

Schwartz asked and patted Steve on the shoulder.

"He patted me on the shoulder!" Steve shouted. "He called me old man!" Then he fainted again.

Bruce the milkman explained, "He's a big fan of yours."

"I didn't know I had any fans left," Sergeant Schwartz said. "I haven't worked in years."

Sergeant Schwartz of the Yukon and Bruce the milkman led Steve to a chair and lowered him into it. He was muttering, "Right here in my store — Sergeant Schwartz of the Yukon — right here — it's too much — too much."

Sergeant Schwartz's real name was Pierre Beeswax. He was an actor who played the famous mountie on television; but there was no explaining that to Steve, who insisted he was nobody other than his hero Sergeant Schwartz.

Outside the Magic Moscow there was a really gaudy panel truck. It was bright red and really shiny, with gold trim and a picture of an Alaskan Malamute. In gold letters on the side of the truck were the words

---

HERCULES, GREAT DOG OF THE NORTH.

"Mr. Beeswax," I said, "is Hercules out there in the truck?"

Steve was just coming out of his trance. "Hercules? Is he here, too? The great lead dog of the north? Oooh, Sergeant Schwartz, let us see him. I love Hercules. I've got all the comic books, and I've seen all the television shows. Hercules is my favorite actor — after you, of course."

"I'm sure Hercules is a little tired of traveling in the truck," Pierre Beeswax, also known as Sergeant Schwartz of the Yukon, said. "I'll go and get him."

"Norman! Bruce! He's going to get the great dog Hercules!" Steve was really excited. "Norman, put down a bowl of fresh water! Hercules might be thirsty. Maybe we should go and get Edward — he wouldn't want to miss this . . . . . . Ooooooh! Look! Isn't he beautiful!"

Pierre Beeswax/Sergeant Schwartz had opened the back door of the truck and lifted out a big Malamute. He was about fifty pounds overweight. He was smiling, and his tongue was hanging out. It looked as though he didn't have many teeth.

Hercules stumbled around the restaurant, dabbed each of our hands with his tongue, took a drink of water, and thumped to the floor. In a minute he was sleeping.

"Old Hercules is a little bit out of condition," Sergeant Schwartz/Pierre Beeswax said.

"Oh, no! He's beautiful," Steve said. "This is the proudest day of my life. But I'm being rude. These are my friends, Norman Bleistift and Bruce the milkman."

We shook hands with the actor.

"And I'm Steve Nickelson. Now may I offer you some refreshment — my treat, of course."

"I'd be delighted," Schwartz/Beeswax said. "I was just looking at all these handsome signs. What, for example, is a Moron's Delight?"

"My masterpiece!" Steve said. "It's a meal, a snack, and a course in practical nutrition all in one. It would be a supreme honor to make one for you — and one for Hercules, in case he wakes up."

Steve whipped together two Moron's Delights, three times normal size. Beeswax/Schwartz went right to work on his. The great dog Hercules accepted the treat and lapped at it without getting off the floor.

"Mr. Beeswax," I asked, "were you ever a real mountie?"

"An interesting question, young Norman Bleistift," he said. "I *could* have been a real mountie. You see, when the producers of Sergeant Schwartz of the Yukon were looking for an actor to play the role, they wanted someone who met all the physical, mental, and moral requirements of the Northwest Constabulary. In fact, since he was going to portray a Mountie, the actor had to be more like all the mounties than any one mountie could be in real life. He had to embody all that was good, brave, and true about those good, brave, and true men of the north. And they picked me — a good choice, don't you think?"

"The best choice," Steve said. "And the best choice of dog to play Hercules, too."

"In fact, I *am* an honorary mountie," Pierre Beeswax continued, "and I am a natural detective. If my gifts as an actor had not been so great, I might have been a mountie, and I'm sure I would have done at least as well as the character I portrayed."

"Sergeant Schwartz, I have a surprise for you," Steve said. "My dog, who took all the prizes at the dog show, is a grandson of Hercules."

"No fooling?" Beeswax said. "I'd be pleased to meet him."

"He's just out back," Steve said. "I'll go and get him." He started for the back door and paused. "I'm sure if Hercules had been there on time, *he* would have won."

"Naturally," said Pierre Beeswax/Sergeant Schwartz.

We heard Steve whistling and calling in the alley. Then he came back into the Magic Moscow. He was very pale. "Edward is gone!" he said.

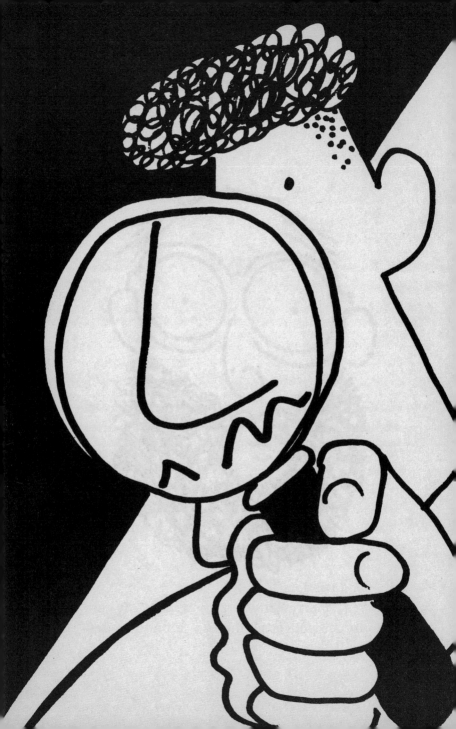

SERGEANT BEESWAX jumped to his feet and rushed out the back door. We all crowded after him. In the alley, he got down on all fours and pulled a magnifying glass out of his back pocket. He examined various scraps of dirt and garbage. Then he jumped to his feet and sniffed the air, licked one finger and held it up to test the wind, and turned to Steve. "Dog rustlers!" he said.

"Dog rustlers?"

"Yes," Pierre Schwartz answered. "My contacts in the police tell me that a band of desperadoes, named Slade, Blackie, and Nick, are operating in this area. I have no doubt that they are the ones who have purloined your prize sled dog. He's worth his weight in gold, you know."

"He is?" Steve asked.

"Certainly," Sergeant Pierre said. "Everybody knows that a dog is man's best friend — well, a good sled dog can mean the difference between life and death on the trail. It is my conviction that these three scoundrels, Nick, Blackie, and Slade, will take your dog to the north country and sell him for a king's ransom."

"Oh, no!" Steve said, "we've got to stop them! Let's call the police!"

"That won't be necessary," Sergeant Schwartz said. "Don't forget, *I* am here. We will pursue them at once."

We hurried through the Magic Moscow. Sergeant Schwartz called to his sleeping dog, "Up, Hercules. Up, you Malamute!" The dog snored. "Oh, drat!" Sergeant Schwartz said, and gathered the huge dog up in his arms and carried him out to the truck, still sleeping. "He's the very devil in a fight," the sergeant said. "If the rascals try to resist, Hercules will be all over them."

Sergeant Schwartz's truck refused to start.

"I'll get my horse!" Bruce the milkman said.

"Good!" Sergeant Schwartz said. "They won't be expecting a horse."

In a few minutes, Bruce the milkman galloped up in the milk wagon. I was impressed. I had never seen Cheryl gallop. In fact, I would never have dreamed that she could gallop.

Hercules was still sleeping off his Moron's Delight. He burped as we transferred him from the back of Sergeant Schwartz's stalled truck to the milk wagon.

"That way! There's no time to lose!" Sergeant Schwartz shouted.

Bruce the milkman clucked his tongue and Cheryl started off at a fast trot. She wasn't about to gallop with three men, a kid, and a fat dog on board.

"How do you know which way they went?" Steve asked.

"Mountie intuition," the sergeant said. "Now keep a sharp lookout. They could be anywhere."

We trotted through the streets of Hoboken. Every now and then, Sergeant Schwartz would say, "Sharp left here!" or, "Turn right, Constable Bruce!" In his excitement, he seemed to think we were all mounties. Sometimes he'd

shout, "On! On, you Malamutes!" In between he'd hum the theme music from the "Sergeant Schwartz of the Yukon" televison show.

"Slade, Nick, and Blackie are masters of disguise," the sergeant said, "and it's possible that they've disguised your dog, too. Don't let anything suspicious escape your notice. It's too bad I don't have my revolver. But we've got Hercules in the back. If they put up a fight, he'll surprise them." Sergeant Schwartz chuckled. Hercules burped.

We only had one false alarm. Sergeant Schwartz stopped a car with four fat ladies in it and accused them of being Slade, Nick, and Blackie with Edward dressed up as a fat lady. Steve managed to calm them down by promising them free Moron's Delights at the Magic Moscow.

Then we sighted Edward! He was trotting down the street, following a little girl who was eating a tuna-fish sandwich as she walked.

Bruce the milkman reined Cheryl to a stop, and Sergeant Schwartz leaped out of the wagon.

"So Blackie, Slade, and Nick are working with an accomplice!" the sergeant said. "Clever of them to use a little girl. Stand still, little girl," he bellowed. "Don't go for your gun, I warn you."

Steve grabbed Edward and put him in the milk wagon. Hercules opened one eye, looked at his grandson, and went back to sleep.

Edward hopped into his customary seat and barked hello to his friend, Cheryl.

Sergeant Schwartz warned the little girl to give up her life of crime. He tried to get her to tell him where Nick, Slade, and Blackie were hiding, but she wouldn't talk. She just chewed on her tuna-fish sandwich and looked at the sergeant as if he were crazy.

Finally we went back to the Magic Moscow.

The four fat ladies Sergeant Schwartz had tried to arrest were there waiting for their free Moron's Delights.

The sergeant, Hercules, and Edward all had Moron's Delights, too, while Bruce the

milkman found the loose wire in Sergeant Schwartz's truck and got it started.

Finally, everybody shook hands: Steve, Bruce the milkman, me, Sergeant Schwartz, the four fat ladies, and Edward. Hercules had dozed off the middle of his second Moron's Delight and had to be carried to the truck.

Sergeant Schwartz loaded Hercules into the front seat and climbed in beside him. "Hercules," he said to the half-asleep dog, "this case is closed."

Then Sergeant Schwartz switched on a tape deck, which played the theme music from the "Sergeant Schwartz of the Yukon" television show, put the truck into gear, and drove off into the sunset over Jersey City.

overleaf: the girl with
the tuna sandwich